WHY IS DAD SO MAD?

BY SETH KASTLE
ILLUSTRATED BY KARISSA GONZALEZ–OTHON

Copyright © 2015 by Seth Kastle
All rights reserved.
Published by Tall Tale Press, 308 E. 19th Street, Hays, KS 67601
All associated logos are trademark of Tall Tale Press and Kastle Books

Printed in the United States of America

First Printing, 2015

ISBN 978-0692402689

www.TallTalePress.com
www.KastleBooks.com

TO MY FAMILY, MY SUPPORT NETWORK, AND MOST IMPORTANTLY
TO JULIE, RAEGAN, AND KENNEDY. I LOVE YOU MORE THAN I CAN
EVER EXPLAIN. WITHOUT YOU IN MY LIFE NOTHING I DO WOULD BE
POSSIBLE. —SETH KASTLE

MOM, WHY IS DAD SO MAD
ALL THE TIME?

HE WAS MAD AT ME TODAY
FOR PLAYING TOO LOUD.

HE WAS MAD AT ME IN THE CAR FOR FIGHTING WITH MY SISTER.

DAD WAS DIFFERENT WHEN HE CAME HOME FROM OVERSEAS.

WHILE HE WAS AWAY, HE HAD TO
DO A LOT OF REALLY HARD,
DANGEROUS WORK.

IT MADE HIM DIFFERENT
THAN HE USED TO BE.

DAD USED TO BE VERY CALM   AND WOULD NEVER GET MAD.

BUT NOW HE HAS TROUBLE RELAXING

OR BEING PATIENT.

NOW, HE GETS ANGRY FAST.

IT'S LIKE DAD ALWAYS HAS A
FIRE
INSIDE HIS CHEST.

WHEN HE GETS MAD, THE FLAME
GROWS AND GROWS REALLY QUICKLY.

WHEN HE GETS MAD,
IT'S LIKE THE FIRE IS IN CONTROL OF HIM.

WHEN DAD YELLS AND IS MAD,
IT'S NOT BECAUSE HE WANTS TO MAKE
YOU FEEL SAD.
HE WOULD DO ANYTHING
NOT TO BE THE WAY HE IS.

BUT THE FIRE IS PART OF WHO HE IS NOW.

SOMETIMES, DAD CAN'T SLEEP. OR HE HAS BAD DREAMS.
THIS MAKES HIM UPSET, TOO.

SOMETIMES, DAD HAS A REALLY HARD TIME REMEMBERING THINGS.

SOMETIMES, DAD NEEDS SOME TIME ALONE TO LET THE FIRE GO OUT,
OR JUST CLEAR HIS MIND.

DAD
LOVES
YOU MORE THAN ANYTHING IN THE WORLD.

JUST BECAUSE HE GETS MAD EASILY,
DOESN'T MEAN HE DOESN'T CARE ABOUT
YOUR FEELINGS.

THINK ABOUT THE TIMES WHEN DAD WRESTLES WITH YOU.

HOW ABOUT WHEN DAD TAKES CARE OF YOU WHEN YOU'RE SICK?

THINK OF ALL THE FUN THINGS

YOU AND YOUR DAD

DO TOGETHER.

DAD AND MOM SOMETIMES
FIGHT A LOT NOW.

BUT WE STILL LOVE EACH OTHER.

SINCE WE ARE A MILITARY FAMILY, WE ARE DIFFERENT THAN OTHER FAMILIES.

SOMETIMES, DAD IS GONE A LOT, AND THAT IS SOMETHING THAT IS HARD FOR ALL OF US.

WE ALL GET
UPSET SOMETIMES

WHEN THINGS
AREN'T THE WAY

WE WOULD LIKE
THEM TO BE.

DAD JUST HAS A REALLY
SHORT FUSE NOW
AND CAN'T ALWAYS BE OK WITH THE
NORMAL HICCUPS WITH LIFE.

JUST KNOW THAT BOTH MOM AND DAD

LOVE YOU

AND

EACH OTHER

MORE THAN ANYTHING.

SOMETIMES, LIFE ISN'T PERFECT. BUT
WE ARE A FAMILY, AND WE WILL
STICK TOGETHER AND

LOVE

EACH OTHER FOREVER.

SETH KASTLE IS THE AUTHOR OF THE CHILDREN'S BOOK WHY IS DAD SO MAD? AND THE UPCOMING WHY IS MOM SO MAD?. BOTH OF THESE BOOKS WERE WRITTEN IN ORDER TO ASSIST MILITARY FAMILIES WHO ARE STRUGGLING WITH PTSD.

SETH RETIRED AFTER A 16 YEAR MILITARY CAREER AS A COMPANY FIRST SERGEANT. HE WAS DEPLOYED IN JANUARY 2002 TO QATAR, AND THEN TO AFGHANISTAN FOR A TOTAL OF EIGHT MONTHS. HE WAS THEN DEPLOYED TO IRAQ IN JANUARY 2003 UNTIL APRIL 2004. HE HAS BEEN MARRIED FOR NEARLY TEN YEARS NOW TO HIS WIFE JULIA, AND HAS TWO DAUGHTERS: RAEGAN AND KENNEDY. HE WROTE THE BOOK WHY IS DAD SO MAD? TO TRY TO HELP HIS CHILDREN UNDERSTAND WHY HE IS THE WAY HE IS NOW. THE OVERRIDING PURPOSE OF THESE BOOKS IS TO LET CHILDREN OF SERVICES MEMBERS KNOW THAT NO MATTER WHAT, THEIR PARENTS LOVE THEM MORE THAN ANYTHING, DESPITE THE CHALLENGES THAT ARE FACED. SETH RESIDES IN KANSAS WHERE HE IS A PROFESSOR OF LEADERSHIP STUDIES AT FORT HAYS STATE UNIVERSITY.

MORE INFORMATION ON SETH AND THESE BOOKS CAN BE FOUND AT WWW.KASTLEBOOKS.COM.

CPSIA information can be obtained
at www.ICGtesting.com
Printed in the USA
LVHW071541180521
687782LV00001B/28

9 780692 402689